Fuchsia FIERCE

Written by

CHRISTIANNE JONES

Illustrated by

KELLY CANBY

Curioux Fox
a capstone imprint

FUCHSIA FIERCE

was a bold name for a little girl.

But Fuchsia wasn't
BOLD OR FIERCE.
She was quiet, shy, tiny and timid.

She was scared to try new things
or stand out in a crowd.

"I know you're scared," her mum said. "But you will love **SUMMER CLUB**."

"Okay," Fuchsia said, but her stomach hurt just thinking about it.

Upon arrival, Fuchsia quickly decided she wasn't
going to let Summer Club change her.
She would do what she always did —

**MAKE UP
EXCUSES**

so she didn't have to
try anything new.

For a while, it worked.

Fuchsia, it's time for swimming.

I forgot my swimming costume.

Then you can sit and watch your friends.

By the end of the week, Fuchsia was running out of excuses and getting bored. Everyone else was having

SO MUCH FUN.

EXCUSES

On game night, Fuchsia saw the
perfect chance to end her boredom.

When her turn rolled around,
everyone was ready for
another excuse.

WORDS

But that excuse never came.
Instead, Fuchsia took a deep breath ...

...AND WALKED TO THE FRONT OF THE ROOM!

Fuchsia was nervous, but nobody laughed.
They shouted out answers and cheered.
It wasn't embarrassing — it was amazing!

After that, Fuchsia started
to try new things —

even if they were
hard or scary.

Was she the best at everything she tried?

NOPE.

But that was okay.

With every activity,
Fuchsia's confidence grew.

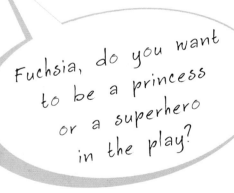

Fuchsia, do you want to be a princess or a superhero in the play?

"I will be a
SUPERHERO PRINCESS!"

She even learned that being tiny
wasn't such a bad trait.

And when Fuchsia called home,
she had a lot to say.

"I love football and horse riding, but not tennis.

I'm trying to learn to play the guitar, but it is really hard.

It turns out I'm good at building things.

I still can't do a cartwheel, but I'm going to keep trying.

And most of all, I'm having fun!"

At times, Fuchsia still felt
quiet, shy, tiny and timid.

But she learned to be brave and strong
and fearless, too. She learned to
BELIEVE IN HERSELF.

She learned that Fuchsia Fierce
really could be

FIERCE.

To Lalayna, Lola and Hattie.
Be bold. Be fierce. Be fearless. Be happy. —C.J.

To Angie, Elizabeth, Annabel, Amelia, Ashleigh and Tess.
Move mountains. —K.C.

First published in 2016 by Curious Fox,
an imprint of Capstone Global Library Limited
264 Banbury Road, Oxford, OX2 7DY – Registered company number: 6695582
www.curious-fox.com

978-1-782-02584-9
20 19 18 17 16
10 9 8 7 6 5 4 3 2

A CIP catalogue for this book is available from the British Library.

Printed and bound in China.